HURRAY FOR HAMTON!

By Linda Aber
Illustrated by John Costanza

A Golden Book • New York
Western Publishing Company, Inc., Racine, Wisconsin 53404

MCMXC

For the rest of the day Buster and Hamton were hard at work. Babs Bunny peeked into the gym and couldn't believe what she saw.

"One two, one two, lift and down, lift and down." Buster was coaching Hamton.

And as Buster called out the count, Hamton lifted a barbell with a one-ton weight on each end.

"Wow!" said Babs. "I never knew Hamton was so strong!"

Buster leaned over and whispered something to Babs. Then she ran off to tell Max what she had just seen Hamton doing.

Pretty soon the whole school had heard about Hamton's amazing strength. Max decided he had to go see this for himself. He hid behind a post and watched Hamton in training. First, Max saw Hamton lift a giant boulder with one hand. "Amazing!" thought Max.

Next, Max watched as Hamton did a quick karate chop on a ten-inch-thick board. The board snapped in half. "His hand doesn't even seem to hurt!" Max said to himself.

Finally, Max saw the most amazing thing of all. Hamton ran with his head down right into a brick wall! The wall crumbled, but Hamton didn't seem to feel a thing.

"This might not be as easy as I thought it was going to be," thought Max. "I don't know how he does it, but that pig packs a powerful punch!"

Max was worried now that he was sure he would lose the fight. He needed time to think.

Max was not the only one worried about the boxing match. Hamton was worried, too. "I don't think I can go through with this," he said.

Just then Hamton's own hero came into the gym. It was Porky Pig. He was there to give Hamton his best advice. "You have nothing to fear but fear itself," said Porky.

"Is that why I'm so scared?" asked Hamton.

Porky Pig tried and tried to help Hamton have the courage to stand up to Max. "But," said Buster, "if my guess is right, there won't be any fight."

Buster was right. At that moment Max came into the gym with an announcement. "The fight is off!" he said. "I've decided it just wouldn't be fair to pick on a poor defenseless pig, and I do mean *poor*. I'll let you go this time but next time I won't be so nice."

As word spread that Max, who had all the ticket money, had called off the match, everyone started to yell, "Refund! Refund! Where is that Max?" But Max had left school quickly.

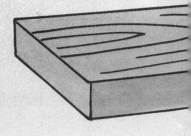

Meanwhile, back in the gym, Porky Pig said, "I told you there was nothing to fear but fear itself."

"You should have told that to Max," said Buster as he easily lifted the boulder in one hand and tossed it up into the air. "I guess we won't be needing these stage props from last week's play anymore. Give me a hand with this stuff, will you?"

With that, Porky Pig, Buster, and Hamton easily carried the boulder, the barbells, the bricks, and the board back to the prop room where they had gotten them. "These things may all be fake," said Buster to Hamton, "but you're a real hero."

"I am?" said Hamton.

"Sure," said Porky. "Now Max won't dare pick a fight with anyone so quickly again."

As Buster and Hamton shook hands for a job well done, Plucky Duck and Babs came in with a surprise.

"A hero for a hero!" said Plucky as he presented Hamton with a giant hero sandwich.

"Next to you, Porky, this is the kind of hero I like best!" Hamton said with a laugh.

"Mmmm, where should I begin?" said Hamton thoughtfully. He was sitting in the Acme Looniversity cafeteria looking at the giant pile of hero sandwiches on the table. "This book says it is important to eat right. So, I guess I'll start on the right!"

As he was eating, Hamton was thinking that the cafeteria was his favorite place in the whole school. This was the place where he always saw his favorite foods and his favorite friends. Then he remembered it was also the place where he saw some people who were not exactly his favorites. One of those people was Montana Max, the richest boy in the school. Max was also the boy who gave Hamton the most problems. Hamton looked up from his lunch and saw Max heading his way.

"Well, well, Hamton, my portly pal," said Max, looking at Hamton and his heap of heros. "I see you're having a little snack there for lunch. That many sandwiches should hold you for about a minute and a half." Max laughed at his own joke. Then he lifted the silver covers off of his own food.

Max didn't wait for an answer. "Tickets go on sale right here, right now!" he announced. "Come see the big boxing match, Montana Max against Hamton! Buy your tickets here!"

Max was right. The money poured in, Hamton's nerves gave out. "Now what do I do?" he asked Plucky.

"You eat," said Plucky, handing Hamton the last sandwich. "And don't worry. Even if you didn't really wrestle the Masked Masher or catch two robbers, you're still a hero to me, Hamton, and I know you'll do just fine." Plucky patted Hamton on the back. Then he left him alone with his sandwich and his troubles.

Hamton was just about to answer Max when Plucky Duck joined them and came quacking to Hamton's defense. "Did you say clothes make the man?" Plucky challenged Max. "Haven't you ever heard the expression, 'You are what you eat'? Even if he doesn't eat all those hero sandwiches, Hamton is already a hero in my eyes."

"Perfect!" said Max as he sniffed the meat on his plate. "Filet mignon for one on this plate and baked Alaska on the other. It's the perfect lunch for a wealthy, healthy, growing boy!" He took another look at Hamton's lunch and said, "I guess your lunch is perfect, too. It's perfect for a growing pig, I mean!"

Hamton tried to pretend that he didn't even hear Max. Instead of saying anything back, Hamton just took another bite of a hero.

"I suppose you think that if you eat hero sandwiches, you'll really become a hero, eh, my roly-poly piglet?" Max teased. "Remember, it's clothes that make the man, not food."

Plucky had heard just about enough out of Max. He jumped up on a table beside his friend and began his defense of Hamton. "Oh, yeah?" said Plucky to Max. "Well maybe you just haven't heard about the time old Hamton here caught the two bank robbers. He was incredible!"

"I was?" said Hamton.

"Incredible," continued Plucky. "Before he was done with that terrible twosome, he threw them both in a garbage can and sat on them until the police came!"

"I am?" said Hamton. "Gee, thanks, Plucky. I never knew you felt that way about me."

"Sure I do, Hamton," Plucky said.

"More important," interrupted Max, "is why you feel that way. What has Hamton ever done to make anyone think he's a hero? He's not even rich!"

"I did?" said Hamton. He was more amazed than anyone in the crowd that had gathered to hear Plucky talk.

"Or how about the time Hamton wrestled against the famous Masked Masher? That guy didn't stand a chance against Hamton!" Plucky was getting a little carried away with his stories. And Hamton was getting more than a little nervous.

Max didn't believe a word of Plucky's stories of Hamton's great courage. "But," he thought to himself, "this could be the perfect opportunity for me to make a little money. No, make that a *lot* of money!"

Max had a plan. Right there, with everyone listening, Max challenged Hamton to a boxing match after school.

"Me?" gulped Hamton nervously. "Box against you?"

It didn't take Hamton long to find Buster. He was standing at his locker listening to all the other kids talk about the big boxing match after school. Hamton quickly pulled Buster to the side and explained what had happened.

"Don't worry about a thing," said Buster. "I'll take charge of your training and the fight will be over even before it begins. Just follow me."

"Me a hero?" thought Hamton. "That's the biggest joke I've ever heard. And this is the biggest mess I've ever been in." Hamton looked at his sandwich. "Now I'm almost too worried to eat," he said to himself. "Well, almost," he said out loud as he took a big bite. Then Hamton had an idea of his own.

"Buster Bunny can get me out of this," Hamton thought. "He always has good advice." Hamton, taking what was left of lunch with him, went to find Buster.